Goodnight, Goodnight, Construction Site

Goodnight, Goodnight, Construction Site

SHERRI DUSKEY RINKER AND TOM LICHTENHELD

chronicle books · san francisco

Down in the big construction site,
The tough trucks work with all their might
To build a building, make a road,
To get the job done—load by load!

The sun has set, the work is done;
It's time for trucks to end their fun.
So one by one they'll go to bed
To yawn and rest their sleepy heads,
Then wake up to another day
Of rough-and-tough construction play!

Working hard to help his team,
Crane Truck raises one last beam.

Reaching, stretching, lifting high,
He swings the beam into the sky.
He'll set it down right on its mark,
Then off to bed; it's almost dark.

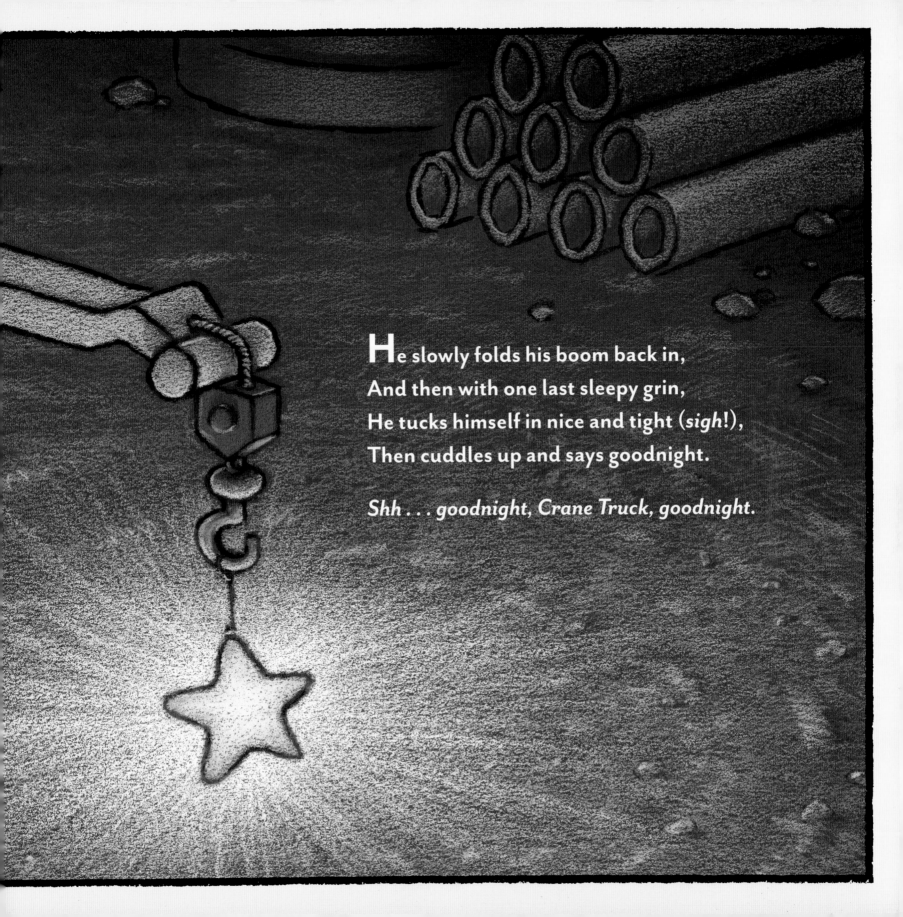

He slowly folds his boom back in,
And then with one last sleepy grin,
He tucks himself in nice and tight (*sigh!*),
Then cuddles up and says goodnight.

Shh . . . goodnight, Crane Truck, goodnight.

Spinning, churning all day long,
Cement Mixer sings his whirly song.

Now (*yawn!*) he's weary

and so dizzy,

From the fun that keeps him busy.

With one last spin, he pours the load.
He's ready now to leave the road.

He takes a bath, gets shiny-bright,
Pulls up his chute, turns off his light.

He cuts his engine, slows his drum,
And dreams sweet dreams of twirly fun.

Shh . . . goodnight, Cement Mixer, goodnight.

Dump Truck loves to work and haul.   He carries loads both big . . .

He moves the dirt
from place to place,
Then dumps it with
a happy face.

. . . and small,

One final load spills on
the heap (*crrrunch!*);
Now Dump Truck's tired
and wants to sleep.

He lowers his bed, locks his gate,
Rests his wheels; it's getting late.
He dims his lights, then shuts his doors,
And soon his engine slows to snores.

Shh . . . goodnight, Dump Truck, goodnight.

Pushing with his mighty blade,
Bulldozer works to smooth the grade.
He clears the way to level ground,
And fills the air with thunderous sound
(*rooaaar!*).

No one's as tough
and strong as he,
But now he's sleepy

as

can

be.

He puffs some smoke

out of his stack,

Turns off his engine,

stops his track.

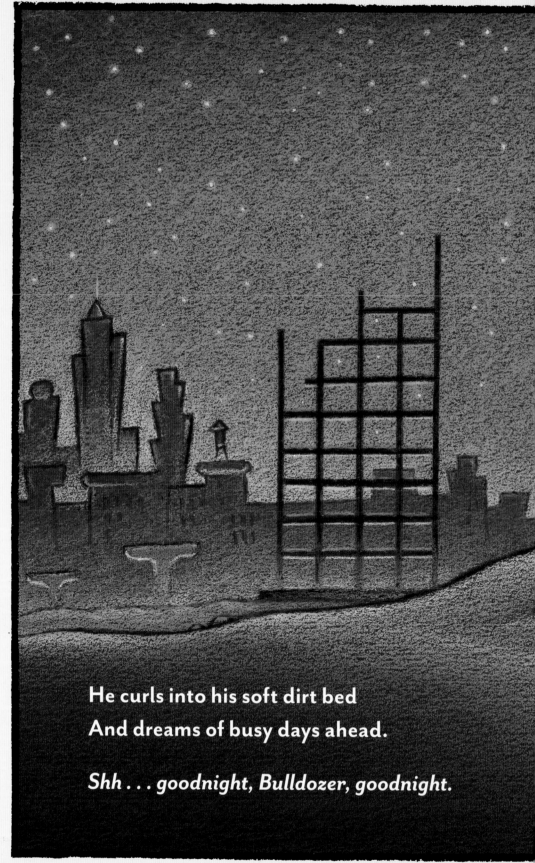

He curls into his soft dirt bed
And dreams of busy days ahead.

Shh . . . goodnight, Bulldozer, goodnight.

Scooping gravel, dirt, and sand,
Excavator shapes the land.
He digs and lifts throughout the day (*arrgh!*),
But now it's time to end his play.

A few more holes to dig and soon
He'll roll to bed beneath the moon.

He twirls upon his bumpy track,
Pulls up his boom, stretches his back.
He sets his scoop down on the ground
And snuggles up without a sound.

Shh . . . goodnight, Excavator, goodnight.

These big, big trucks, so tough and loud,
They work so hard, so rough, and proud.
Tomorrow is another day,
Another chance to work and play.

Turn off your engines, stop your tracks,
Relax your wheels, your stacks, and backs.
No more huffing and puffing, team:
It's time to rest your heads and dream.

Construction site, all tucked in tight,
The day is done, turn off the light.

Great work today! Now . . . shh . . . goodnight.

For one blue-eyed boy and one brown-eyed boy and the world of wonder and possibility I see through their eyes. And, always, for Faith. —S. R.

To Jan, for sharing a dream. —T. L.

First paperback special edition published in 2017 by Chronicle Books LLC.
Originally published in hardcover in 2011 by Chronicle Books LLC.

Text © 2011 by Sherri Duskey Rinker.
Illustrations © 2011 by Tom Lichtenheld.

ISBN 978-1-4521-6955-2

The Library of Congress has cataloged the original edition as follows:
Rinker, Sherri Duskey.
Goodnight, goodnight, construction site / by Sherri Duskey Rinker ;
illustrated by Tom Lichtenheld.
p. cm.
Summary: At sunset, when their work is done for the day, a crane truck, a cement mixer, and other pieces of construction equipment make their way to their resting places and go to sleep.
ISBN 978-0-8118-7782-4 (alk. paper)
[1. Stories in rhyme. 2. Construction equipment—Fiction. 3. Trucks—Fiction.]
I. Lichtenheld, Tom, ill. II. Title.
PZ8.3.R48123Goo 2011
[E]—dc22
2010025008

Manufactured in China.

Typeset in Mr. Eaves.
The illustrations in this book were rendered in oil pastels on Mi-Teintes paper.

10 9 8 7 6 5 4 3

Chronicle Books LLC
680 Second Street, San Francisco, California 94107

Chronicle Books—we see things differently.
Become part of our community at
www.chroniclekids.com